Pirate Pete
keeps fit

Written by Susan Akass

Illustrated by Ben Cort

Pete was a pirate.

He had a parrot called Beaky.

Pete had a big tummy.

One day Pete said to Beaky,
'I can't do up my trousers.
My tummy is too big.'

'I don't like my big tummy,'
said Pete.
'What can I do?'

'I will help you,' said Beaky.
'Do what I do.'

Beaky ran up and down.
Pete ran up and down.

Beaky jumped up and down.
Pete jumped up and down.

'I want to stop now,' said Pete.

'No,' said Beaky.

'You can't stop.'

Pete ran up and down
and up and down.

He jumped up and down
and up and down.

'Can I stop now?' said Pete.
'Yes, you can,' said Beaky.

'Now my tummy is not too big,'
said Pete.
'I can do up my trousers.'
'Oh no!' said Beaky.

'Thundering Cannonballs!'
said Pete.